Frankenstein

by Mary Shelley

Retold by Alison Leonard

Illustrated by Mike Perkins

ies Editors: Steve Barlow and Steve Skidmore

Published by Ginn and Company
Halley Court, Jordan Hill, Oxford OX2 8EJ
A division of Reed Educational and Professional Publishing Ltd
Telephone number for ordering **Impact**: 01865 888084

OXFORD MELBOURNE AUCKLAND JOHANNESBURG
BLANTYRE GABORONE IBADAN PORTSMOUTH (NH)
USA CHICAGO

First published 1999

2003 2002 2001 2000

10 9 8 7 6 5 4 3 2

ISBN 0 435 21259 1

Illustrations
Mike Perkins

Cover artwork
Chris Swee / The Organisation

Designed by Shireen Nathoo Design

Printed and bound in Great Britain by Biddles

Contents

Who was Frankenstein?

Was he a man or a monster?

He was a man.

Forget the films.

Forget everything you have heard.

This is the story of Victor Frankenstein.

He was a scientist.

It is also the story of **Elizabeth**, the woman who loved him,

of their friend **Henry**,

and of Victor's young brother, **William**.

It is the story of someone else, too.

But that comes later...

Chapter 1
The strike of lightning

Victor Frankenstein was born in Switzerland. He grew up to love snowy mountains, green valleys and dark forests.

Victor was an only child. But he had a friend called Elizabeth, whose parents were dead. Elizabeth was beautiful and got on well with everyone.

When Victor was thirteen, his parents had a second child, called William. They were a happy family. They often met up with Elizabeth and another friend, Henry.

Henry wrote stories and loved parties. Victor tried to join in the fun. But usually he was thinking about his big ambition. He wanted to be a scientist.

When Victor was about to leave school, a terrible storm struck the mountains near his home. The family huddled by a window to watch the lightning and listen to the thunder.

Victor was excited. He knew lightning was electric. Electricity was powerful enough to kill. Could it also bring something alive?

Then he had his great idea. "I'll create a human being and bring it to life!"

Victor was getting ready to go to University, when something dreadful happened. Both Victor's parents caught a fever. Doctors could not help them.

Lying on her deathbed, Victor's mother said to Victor and Elizabeth, "Promise me you'll take care of each other."

When Victor went off to University, Henry and Elizabeth took him there.

"You're lucky to be studying science, Victor," said Henry. "Maybe you'll find out how to cure fever."

But Victor had other ideas. He wanted to find the secret of life and death.

CHAPTER 2
Pieces of death

Victor was a brilliant student. But every night, after his studies, he started his real work.

He stole dead bodies from graveyards and tombs.

He took them to a small hut hidden in a dark forest. This hut was his laboratory.

He cut the bodies into tiny pieces. Then he stitched them together to make a new person.

Victor didn't mind being alone. He wasn't put off by the smell or the touch of dead bodies.

He would be like God, the creator of new life. He had a picture in his mind of the Creature he was making. It would be beautiful, wise and good.

But, as he worked, Victor found he had a problem.

He wanted to make a Creature of normal size. But his fingers were too big and clumsy to work with small parts. He had to use bigger pieces.

His Creature wouldn't be beautiful, as he'd hoped. It would be a terrifying giant.

But Victor tried not to think about it. He thought of nothing except finishing his secret task. On and on he worked, putting together each bone, each piece of gut, each muscle, each blood vessel and cell.

He forgot all about Elizabeth, Henry and William. They were worried about him. They wrote letters asking when they would see him again.

But Victor didn't write back. He worked on until he had finished his Creature.

Chapter 3
It lives!

Now Victor had only one task left. To bring the Creature to life.

He had never forgotten the way lightning had struck the oak tree in the garden. He needed to find a way to use the power of electricity.

After days and nights of hard work, he found out how he could give life to his Creature.

Victor was thrilled. He imagined what the newspapers would say about him.

VICTOR FRANKENSTEIN, THE MAN WHO DISCOVERED THE SECRET OF LIFE.

The world of science today has a new genius. Victor Frankenstein is still only a student. But he has discovered how to put life into a body made out of dead parts. Things will never be the same again…

But Victor was also terrified. No one had ever done this before. No one knew what a Creature like his might do!

He stopped work and went back to study in the town.

But he knew he couldn't stop now. He must finish what he had begun.

On a dreary night in November, Victor went back to his laboratory.

There lay his lifeless Creature. It was waiting for the spark that would make it breathe, move and speak.

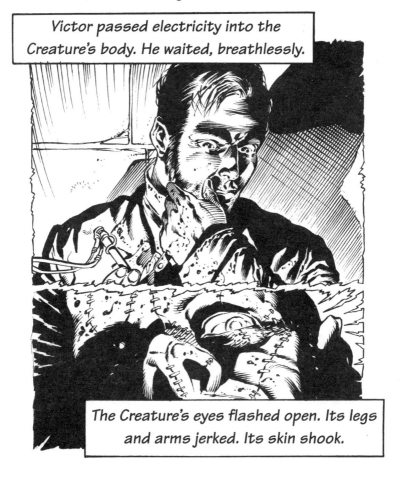

Victor passed electricity into the Creature's body. He waited, breathlessly.

The Creature's eyes flashed open. Its legs and arms jerked. Its skin shook.

17

This wasn't what Victor wanted! People would hate him now! He threw off his lab coat and raced away through the forest.

He decided to go to his friend, Henry, and tell him everything. Henry was a writer. He understood people's feelings. Victor ran till he reached Henry's house.

When he got there, he collapsed.

"Victor!" cried Henry. "What's happened? You're ill. Come in and rest."

Victor realised he had been crazy to think Henry would understand. How could anyone understand?

"Yes, I'm ill," he said, and stumbled upstairs.

But at the bedroom door, he stopped.

What if the Creature was waiting for him?

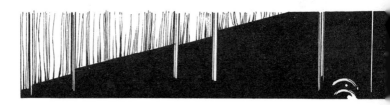

Shaking from head to foot, he turned the handle and pushed open the door.

The room was empty.

Henry came up the stairs behind him.

"Victor! You look as if you've seen a ghost! I'll look after you till you're better. Elizabeth is hoping that you and she might be married soon."

But Victor couldn't think about marriage. His mind was filled with only one thing – the dreadful face of his Creature.

Chapter 4
Giant child

Back in the hut, high in the forest, the
Creature had sat up as Victor ran out.
Blinking his eyes, he looked around.

He was huge and ugly. But he didn't know it. Although he was bigger than an adult, he had the mind of a child.

Slowly he got used to the light. He looked at things till they took shape. He felt the hardness of the bench he was sitting on. He sniffed the strange smells of the room. He heard the sound of birds outside.

Carefully getting off the bench, he picked up the lab coat. He put it on and wobbled to the door. He stepped outside and started to walk.

Gazing around him, he saw how the land rose in tall, white peaks. He realised that the sun made him warm and the trees gave him shelter. He found water in the streams, and shivered when darkness came.

Then he fell into a deep sleep.

When he woke up, he saw the cool, silver moon in the sky. He shivered again, and knew he must find a way to keep warm.

He walked down the mountain until he saw some houses. Nearby was a bonfire.

"Ah!" he thought. "It's warm."

He thrust his hand into the fire, but quickly pulled it out again. He couldn't understand why it hurt so much.

He was very hungry. "Maybe the people here will give me food," he thought.

But the people were terrified when they saw the Creature coming. They ran away, screaming for help.

The Creature was puzzled. Why did people think he would hurt them? He only wanted food, warmth and friendship. Tired and lonely, he wandered on into a wood.

The next day he saw a cottage, all on its own. No one had seen him. He decided to hide, and see what happened.

First a young man and woman came out. They looked kind, but they were thin and poor.

Then an old man stumbled out. The young woman went back to help him. Something was wrong with the old man's eyes.

The Creature didn't want the family to be scared.

From his hiding place, he saw how they grew vegetables and caught rabbits to eat. He watched as they collected firewood and cooked meals.

The Creature learned to do the same. Secretly, he helped them. Each morning they found more firewood than the night before. On the doorstep they found fruit, or a rabbit for the pot.

He saw how the family talked to each other. He was glad when they laughed. But if they were hungry or in pain, he was upset.

When they were out one day, he crept into the cottage. He looked at their furniture, beds and cooking pots. Then he found something that didn't seem to have any use.

He sniffed it, but it didn't smell. He licked it, but it had no taste. He listened, but it made no sound. He had never seen a book before.

One sunny day the woman sat outside, talking to the old man while she looked at the book. The Creature saw that she was reading to him.

When the cottage was empty again, he crept in. Over time, he learned to read.

The Creature had been wearing the lab coat ever since he left the hut. In the pocket were some papers. Now he could read them.

So, at last, he read the story of how he had been made. He hated every word. He hated the diagrams, the sums and the plans.

Then his despair and rage turned against his creator.

"Why did Victor Frankenstein make me, and then leave me?"

Now he knew the terrible truth, he needed a plan. He would get to know this family. They were living a good and simple life. He must learn to live it, too.

But how could he stop them running away in fear? There was one way. The old man couldn't see him.

"He won't know how ugly I am. I'll make friends with him first, and then he can tell the young people that I mean no harm," the Creature thought.

He waited until the young man and woman had gone into the village and the old man was alone. The Creature was nervous, but he went and knocked on the door.

28

The Creature knew he had to leave before the young couple came back.

As he stood up, the old man said to him, "You might know the answer to a puzzle. Someone has been helping us. Whoever it is must be very strong. He uses no axe on the wood. It's not chopped. It must be broken somehow."

The Creature didn't answer. Instead, he took the biggest log out of the box, and broke it with his bare hands.

At that moment, the young couple returned.

Terrified, the young woman rushed to protect the old man.

The young man picked up a chair and ran at the giant Creature. All three were screaming.

Howling with despair, the Creature ran for his life.

CHAPTER 5
A murder and a hanging

Victor stayed at Henry's house for many weeks. Elizabeth often wrote to him.

Dearest Victor,

I hope you will be better soon.

William is growing up quickly. A girl called Justine has come to help me look after him. She is poor, but from a good family.

We miss you, and hope to see you soon...

Victor was pleased to hear from Elizabeth. But he thought mostly of the Creature he had made. It might be striding around the world, hurting people or killing them!

"What you need now, Victor," said Henry, "is a change of scene and some sunshine. Let's go away."

While they were on holiday, Victor almost forgot about the Creature. But when they got back, a letter from Elizabeth arrived with terrible news.

Dearest Victor,

My heart aches to write this. Your brother, William, is dead. He has been murdered.

William, Justine and I were walking in the forest. William went off on his own. We didn't worry. He knows the forest well.

But as time went by, we became worried. Justine and I went in different directions to look for him. I found him in a clearing in the forest. He was stretched out lifeless on the grass. He had huge marks on his neck. It almost looked as if the murderer was some kind of monster!

Victor's heart thumped. The huge marks could only mean one thing. The killer must be a giant. His Creature!

Again he tried to put the Creature out of his mind. He needed to go to Elizabeth and comfort her. He would ask her to marry him.

He and Henry set out on the journey. Victor wanted to cry because his brother was dead. But he was too frightened for tears.

When they arrived, Elizabeth opened the door. Her eyes were red with weeping. Victor put his arms around her. He remembered his promise to look after her.

"Are they searching for the murderer?" he asked.

Elizabeth tore herself from Victor's arms and cried, "There's no need to search! It could only have been Justine! She came to care for William, but instead she killed him!"

"No!" Victor shouted. "That can't be true!"

"But it is!" replied Elizabeth. "She killed him to steal the locket from around his neck!"

Victor remembered giving the locket to William. It had a portrait of their mother inside.

"Where is the locket now?" he asked.

"They can't find it," replied Elizabeth. "The wicked girl must have hidden it."

"Justine is not the murderer!" cried Victor. "I know who it is! It's… "

But Elizabeth didn't hear what Victor was trying to say. His words were drowned by noises from outside.

People were hammering on the door and shouting, "The hanging! Come and see the hanging! Watch her swing!"

The three of them hurried after the crowds to the village square.

They watched the noose being put around Justine's neck. The people's shouts faded.

Victor opened his mouth. There was only one moment left. He must cry out the words, "This young woman did not kill William! I know who did!"

But he couldn't speak. The words choked in his throat.

Then it was too late.

CHAPTER 6

Make me a mate!

Victor couldn't stay a moment longer. He knew he must find the Creature, and kill him.

"Elizabeth," he said, "I am sorry, I must go away again. I have a task to do."

Elizabeth was horrified. "Surely you can't leave me at a time like this?" she said.

But Victor had no choice. He ran, and didn't stop till he had reached the icy mountains.

Weary and out of breath, he gazed around him. The snowy peaks glittered in the sunlight. A glacier, a stretch of solid ice, lay between him and the mountains.

Suddenly, he saw the figure of a man. It was running at superhuman speed across the ice towards him.

Victor was filled with hate and rage. How evil the Creature looked.

This was his chance! He had made this terrible Creature. Now he would fight him to the death.

"You devil!" cried Victor. "How dare you come near me? Have you no shame?"

The Creature's howl echoed across the ice. "It is you who should feel shame, Victor Frankenstein! How did you dare to play with life?"

"Monster!" shouted Victor. "Come here! I began your evil life. Now I'll put an end to it!"

Step by step, Victor moved over the ice towards his Creature. At last they were close. Victor reached out his hand to grab the Creature, and they stood face to face.

For the first time, Victor looked into the eyes of the Creature he had made. They were filled with fear and pain.

41

Victor laughed scornfully. "What is worse than death?"

"My story is worse than death, and you must listen to it," replied the Creature.

"How can I listen to you? You killed my brother!" Victor shouted.

"Yes," said the Creature. "I did. But let us go down from the mountain, Victor Frankenstein. Then you can hear the terrible story of how it happened."

The Creature led Victor down and they sat on the grassy slopes below. Then the Creature told his story.

"I started off good," he said. "But everyone was frightened of me. Everyone else had someone to love them. I had no one. Then I thought I might have found a friend. A boy ran across my path, playing.

"I thought this child was too young to know about fear, so I tried to talk to him. But he shouted at me.

" 'Victor Frankenstein'. I knew that was the name of my maker. I had to stop him saying that dreadful name!

"I put my hands round his throat to stop him talking.

"In a moment, the child lay dead at my feet.

"I found this locket round his neck. There was a picture of a beautiful woman inside. I was filled with rage. I could tell she must have been your mother.

"She must have loved your father, and he must have loved her.

"But I can never love anyone like that. No one will ever love me. Everyone is afraid of me and hates me!

"I am nearly at the end of my story. But you must listen for a few more moments. There is one task left for you to do."

Victor turned cold with fear. "What task is that?" he asked.

"Make me a mate. Make me a woman who is ugly and hateful to look at. A monster like I am. I promise we will be cut off from everyone else. But because we are cut off, we will be closer to each other. Give me someone to love!"

"I cannot!" cried Victor. "One of you is terrible enough. Two is impossible!"

"If you make me a mate," said the Creature, "we will leave you alone. We will go and live far away. But if you do not… "

"If I do not?" asked Victor, trembling.

"Then I promise that I will destroy you!" cried the Creature.

Victor remembered the good, beautiful Creature he had wanted to make. Could he make a second Creature like that?

Maybe. But what if it was horrible, too?

The day was ending. It was getting dark.
At last Victor felt sadness for the Creature.
Could love change it into something
beautiful?

"I swear that I would," said the Creature.

"Then I will make you a mate," said Victor.

The Creature gave a great cry, and leapt away across the darkening ice.

CHAPTER 7

Terror of the wedding

Victor went home with a heavy heart. He wanted to see Elizabeth before he started his last and most terrible work.

Elizabeth was waiting for him. She was lonely and sad.

"Elizabeth," Victor said. "Let's hope the bad times are over. I want us to be happy together. Will you be my wife?"

"I've never wanted to marry anyone but you," Elizabeth replied. "Yes, Victor, I will."

Henry was pleased when they told him the good news.

"I'm so happy for you both," he said. He took out his diary. "When will the wedding be?" he asked.

"No, not yet!" cried Victor. " I'm sorry. I must ask you to wait just a little longer."

Henry was shocked, and Elizabeth's eyes filled with tears. "Surely you've finished your work now?" she said. "Isn't it time for you to be with me?"

But Victor was already out of the door.

He went back to his hut in the forest. He set up his table and tools. At night, he went secretly to graveyards and tombs, and carried the bodies back.

Just as before, he cut them as small as he could and pieced them together.

Now he had stopped caring if his new creation was an ugly giant. "The uglier the better," he thought. "Then I'll never see them again."

He chewed dry bread as he worked. He didn't stop for sleep. He worked night and day without a break.

As he worked, the Creature was never far away. Sometimes Victor looked up and saw a huge shadow outside the window.

He knew that the Creature was watching.
He began to have second thoughts.

He'd promised to make a mate for the
Creature. But surely it was madness. That
monster had killed his brother!

"I must not do it. I'll break my promise,"
he thought.

So, by the light of the moon, Victor destroyed the half-made body and all his tools. He swept his hut clean of every sign of what he had been doing.

Then he was worn out. He crawled into a corner and slept.

As morning came, he heard a broken voice.

"You have not kept the promise that you made. Now I have nothing to hope for!"

Victor held his breath. He saw the Creature's face at the window, and the voice came again.

Victor ran to the door and out down the mountain. But when he reached the village, something even more terrible was waiting.

A noisy crowd surrounded him. "Here he comes! Victor Frankenstein! Throw him into jail!"

"What's this?" cried Victor. "Jail? Why?"

The people dragged him to the village hall, shouting, "Let him see the corpse! Then let him swing!"

They pushed him through the door. There lay the body of Henry, stretched out dead on the floor.

Chapter 8
The end – or is it?

Victor lay in jail, thinking with horror about his dead friend.

"They want my blood in revenge for Henry's death," he thought. "And once again, I know that my Creature was the real killer!"

Someone knocked softly on the door. The key turned and the door opened. Victor saw the wrinkled face of an old woman.

"Who are you?" asked Victor, shocked.

"I'm the cleaner," whispered the old woman. "I see everything that goes on around here. I saw you working up in the mountains.

"I saw Henry when he came looking for you. He was climbing the mountain.

"But the next day I saw a giant carrying Henry's body across the ice.

"I'll tell the people you didn't kill your friend," said the old woman. "Go now. Run! But find your giant, and make sure he doesn't kill again!"

She pushed Victor out through the door. He escaped, and he never even knew the name of the woman who had saved his life.

Victor knew he must see Elizabeth quickly before he went after the Creature. William, Justine and Henry were dead. Who might be next? He must tell Elizabeth the truth.

Elizabeth was shocked to see Victor free. But Victor was amazed by the letter Elizabeth handed him.

My dear Victor,

   I cannot say these words to your face. I must write
them down and give them to you.

   You have spent so much time away from me. There
can be only one reason. You love another woman.

   You think I will hate you, but I do not. I forgive you.
You must go to her.

   Dear Victor, be happy, as your mother wanted you
to be…

Victor was horrified.

"No, Elizabeth! There is no one for me but you!"

He knelt beside her and held her hand. He pleaded with her to believe him.

"Then why have you been away so long?" she asked.

"I can't explain now," said Victor. "I promise I'll tell you everything after we are married."

But all the time, the voice of the Creature echoed at the back of his mind:

"I will be with you on your wedding night."

The old woman's news that Victor hadn't killed Henry soon spread around the village. For a while Victor was almost at peace.

He knew he must find the Creature before it was too late. But when the day of the wedding finally came, the Creature was still free.

The wedding was a quiet one, with only a few close friends.

Then Victor took Elizabeth to a house high up in the mountains for their honeymoon. He hoped they would be safe there.

He wanted to be sure the Creature hadn't followed them. So he searched every room.

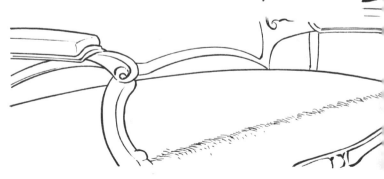

59

Victor went out of the house and walked under the night sky.

Everything was still. The moon and a million stars hung overhead. He remembered the Creature's words, "I promise that I will destroy you."

Suddenly, he heard a piercing scream from the house. It came from the room where he had left Elizabeth.

Victor ran like lightning and saw the sight he had dreaded for so long.

Victor grabbed his pistol and ran downstairs. He raced out of the house, through valleys, over rocks and up the mountain.

A giant figure ran in front of him in the moonlight. Victor fired shots towards him. But the Creature ran on.

It seemed the Creature could run for ever. Victor could not. A terrible pain exploded in his chest.

Defeated at last, Victor fell down in the snow.

As the beat of his heart grew slower and slower, he saw the Creature's terrible face.

"Oh Frankenstein!" said the Creature. "You made me, and now I have caused your death!"

The Creature's last words rang out in the mountains, and echoed back.

Who will be like Frankenstein in the future? Who will look for the secret of life but instead bring death?

ABOUT THE AUTHORS

Alison Leonard first read **Frankenstein** when she wrote a play about Mary Shelley. She says, "I enjoy creating people through my writing." Alison is married and lives in Cheshire. One of her two daughters is a scientist.

Mary Shelley wrote **Frankenstein** nearly 200 years ago, long before people understood electricity and genetics. She was only 19 and had run away from home.

RETELLING
SET D